characters created by lauren child

I absolutely LOVE animals

PUFFIN BOOKS
Published by the Penguin Group: London, New York, Australia,
Canada, India, Ireland, New Zealand and South Africa
Penguin Books Ltd, Registered Offices: 80 Strand, London WC2R 0RL, England

puffinbooks.com

I Completely Know About Guinea Pigs first published 2008
I Will Not Ever Never Forget You, Nibbles first published 2012
This collection first published 2012
001
Made and printed in China
ISBN: 978-0-718-19916-6

I **completely** KNOW about **guinea pigs**

Text based on the script

written by Paul Larson and Laura Beaumont   Illustrations from the TV animation

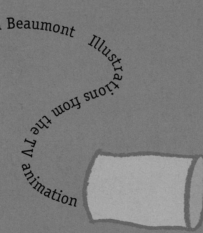

produced by Tiger Aspect

I have this little sister Lola.
She is small and very funny.
At the moment Lola is...
"What ARE you doing at the moment, Lola?"

"I am being a
guinea pig,"
says Lola.

I say, "Why?"

"Because I really like
guinea pigs.
And maybe, if Mrs Hanson
lets me, I can bring Bert, our
class guinea pig, home for
the school holidays."

"Have you asked Mum?"

"Yes," says Lola.
"She said it will be

completely

FINE."

The next day at school, Lola says,
"Lotta, do you know ALL about guinea pigs?"
And Lotta says, "There are lots of DIFFERENT
kinds of guinea pig...

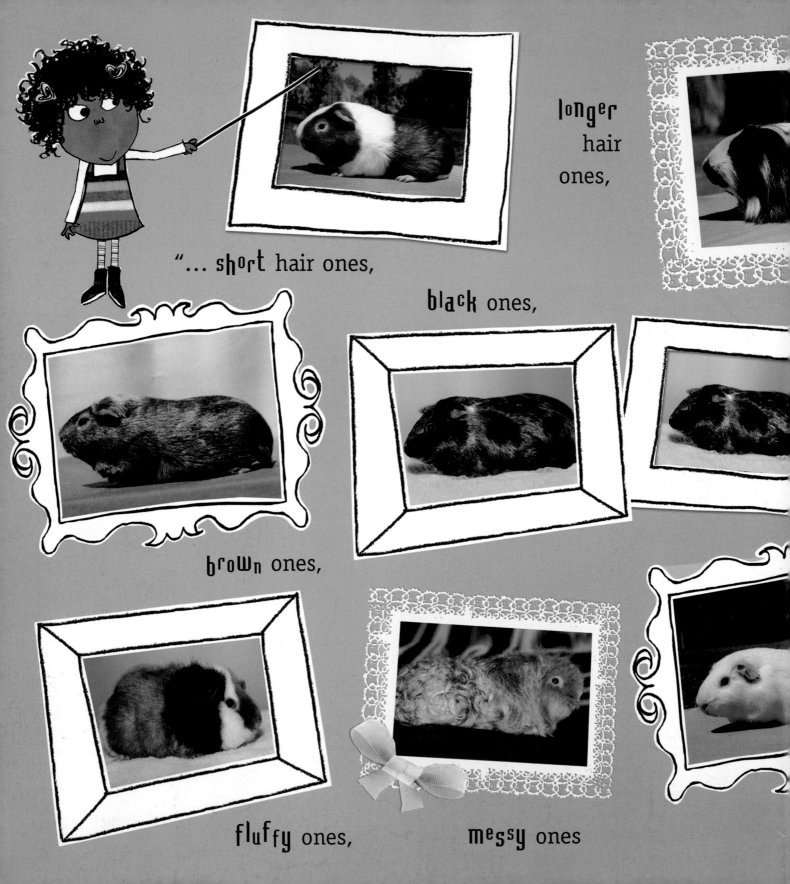

longer
hair
ones,

"... **short** hair ones,

black ones,

brown ones,

fluffy ones,

messy ones

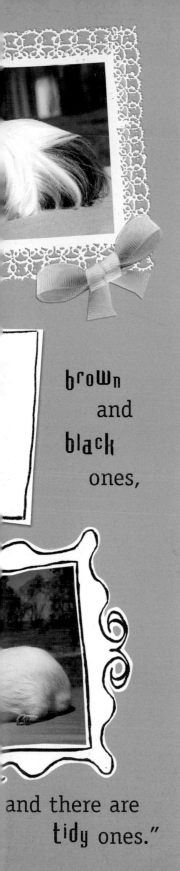

brown
and
black
ones,

and there are
tidy ones."

"I thought Bert was a girl guinea pig,"
says Lola. "He looks
like a girl, because his hair's all pretty."

Mini says, "No, Bert's a boy guinea pig."

"How do you know all
about guinea pigs?" says Lotta.

"Because I've got one at home...
he's called Fluffy and he
comes from Peruuuuuuu."

"Peruuuu?" say Lola and Lotta.

"Where is Peruuuuu?"

"It's a very long way away, and in Peru there is lots of long grass.

Guinea pigs love long grass
because they are shy.

squeak!

"Hello, I'm in Peruuuuuu!"

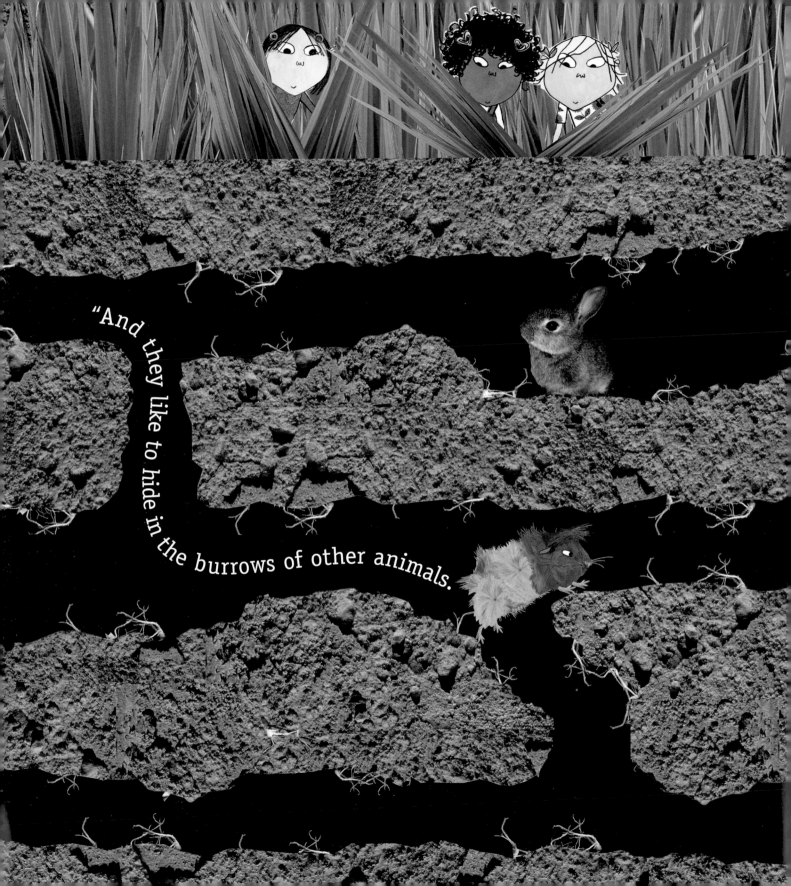

"And they like to hide in the burrows of other animals.

Guinea pigs like to gnaw
on wood and twigs
and things so that
their teeth don't
GROW
really
long.

And they use their whiskers

to see if they can squeeze into...

... different spaces."

Lola says, "I've asked Mrs Hanson if I can take Bert home for the school holidays."

"I've asked Mrs Hanson too," says Bernard. "And I know what they eat!"

"Um... biscuits?"
says Lola.

"No they DON'T, Lola.
Guinea pigs eat
fruit and
vegetables and grass,"
says Mini.

"And
bran,"
says
Bernard.

Lola whispers to Lotta,
"I don't think
Mrs Hanson will choose me
to take Bert home
because they know
everything about
guinea pigs and
I don't."

"Oooh, please pick ME,
please
PICK ME,"
says Lola.

And Lola **does** get picked!
So on the way home I say, "Do you know how to look after Bert?"

"Yes I do, Charlie. Mrs Hanson told me **everything** after the class. She said...

I have to give him clean
water every day

and new straw for his bed,

and he mustn't stay outside
at night-time because it
gets really cold,

and you must ALWAYS
wash your hands after holding him,

and he likes to eat
fruit and vegetables,

but NOT
potatoes, Charlie.

You must never
ever
give a guinea pig
potato...

or crisps."

Then Lola says,
    "And don't you think
Bert looks like a girl?"

    "I don't know," I say.

"Well, I think he looks like
    a girl," says Lola.

"There!
        A bed for Bert.
There you go, Bert!

If you were my very
        OWN guinea pig,

I would always take you
shopping with Mum...

and I would
take you to the
cinema...

"I would
TAKE
you
everywhere!"

Then I say,
    "Do you want to play
Snap with me, Lola?"

        "No thank you,
Charlie. I am stroking
        Bert because I don't
want him to be lonely."

"How could he get
lonely! You haven't
        left him for one
        single moment!"

Later I say,
"Dad has made this for your
guinea pig run!"

"Oh goody!" says Lola.
"My guinea pig run is full of
adventures!

Bert is just going to completely LOVE IT."

"Ready... steady... GO!

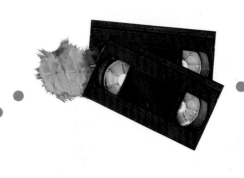

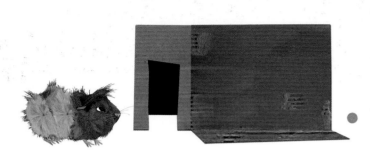

Look, Charlie, look at Bert!

He's going really fast!"

"Bert?

BERT...?

BERT?!

Where is he?

Charlie!

Bert is
completely,
extremely
GONE!"

"Bert?"

"Bert!"

"Maybe he didn't like me," says Lola.
"Maybe he's run away."

And I say, "He hasn't run away.
He has to be here
somewhere."

The next day we STILL

can't find Bert.

"Oh no!
What am I going
to say to Mrs Hanson?"
says Lola.

But then Lola
hears a noise.

"Huh?
Squeaking!"
says Lola.

"It's coming
from over
there..."

"It's
BERT!

And

he's **gone**

all

tiny!"

And I say, "I don't think Bert is a boy, Lola."
"What do you mean?" says Lola.
"I think Bert has had babies."
And Lola says, "I said he was a girl!"

I will not EVER neVer FORGET you, nibbles

Text based on the script written by Anna Starkey   Illustrations from the TV animation produced by Tiger Aspect

I have this little sister Lola.
She is small and very funny.
Today Lola is very excited because Mum and Dad
say I'm allowed to have a pet mouse.

Lola says, "Charlie, why don't you call your **mouse**,
...**Mouse**!"

I say,
"Well, I think I'll call him
Nibbles because he
likes to **chew** things."

"Hello, Nibbles," says Lola.
"Can I please hold him, Charlie?"

And I say,
"Not yet, Lola. The man in the shop said
we have to let him get used to us
and to his new home... slowly."

Nibbles makes lots of noise in his cage.

Lola says, "He's **running** very fast in his wheel, Charlie."

I say, "Mice like to **run** in a wheel, Lola.
It's how they **exercise**."

Every time I **play** with Nibbles, Lola always wants to join in too.

She says,
"Nibbles **really** is EXTREMELY **clever**!

Oooh, make him go up MY arm too, Charlie!"

When it's "Bring a Pet to School" Day,
I take Nibbles with me.

In assembly, I say, "Mice are really clever."
Also, they have tails which are the same length
as their bodies.

Mice use their
whiskers so they
feel where they are.

"I am now going to
show you how **clever**
my **mouse**, Nibbles, is.

My sister, Lola, is going to help me.

You can do it, Nibbles. Go to Lola."

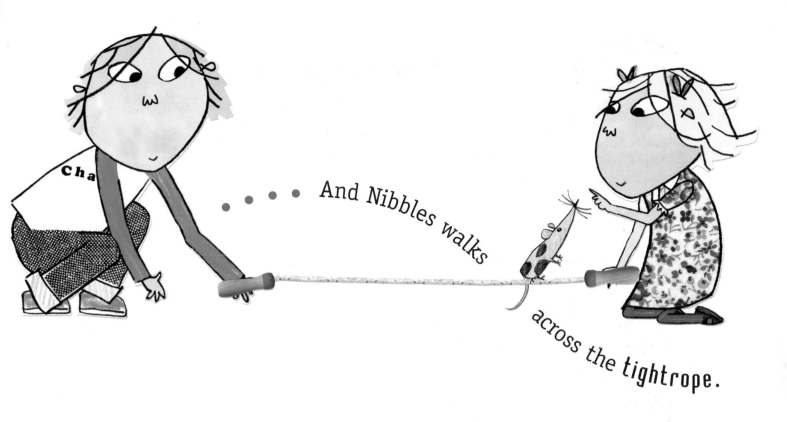

And Nibbles walks across the tightrope.

Lola says,

"Nibbles did it!"

And then Nibbles walks

upside down!

On the way home, I say,
"When Nibbles is older and bigger,
he might be able to do
all kinds of tricks..."

Lola says,
"Yes, millions and
a hundred of people will come
to see Nibbles
the DAREDEVIL mouse."

"He could be the first ever **mouse** to cross a **waterfall** on a tightrope," I say.

I say, "Come on, Nibbles!"

"Yes, come on, Nibbles," says Lola.

Marv says, "Oh, I can't watch!"

"You can DO it!"
says Lotta.

"He's the CLEVEREST
mouse in the universe!"
says Lola.

Lola says, "Nibbles will have to be much
bigger-er to do that trick, won't he, Charlie?"

"Yes, Lola," I say. "He will need to be
more of a GROWN UP mouse."

Nibbles **plays** with me and Lola...

in summer...

and autumn...

and winter...

and he **plays**
with us in spring.

But then one morning I go to wake
Nibbles up and he's very **still**.

Lola says, "Sleepy Nibbles.
Do you think he will wake up if I go
and get his favourite **mouse** food?"

"No, Lola," I say.
"Because I think that Nibbles has died."

Lola says, "I don't think so, Charlie. He is just **tired**."

Then Lola says,
    "Nibbles is completely NOT moving, Charlie."

    So I say, "I'm afraid, Lola,
        that Nibbles is definitely
NOT going to wake up."

Later on, Mum says we can use a **shoebox** to bury Nibbles in.

Lola says, "Why do we have to bury him, Charlie?"

"It's what you do when your mouse dies," I say.
"We could make Nibbles a **sarcophagus**."

"What is a **sar-pop-opus**?" says Lola.

I say, "In Ancient Egypt, when people died,
they were buried in a **sarcophagus**.

Each **sarcophagus** was decorated
and it would be filled with
the person's **favourite** things.

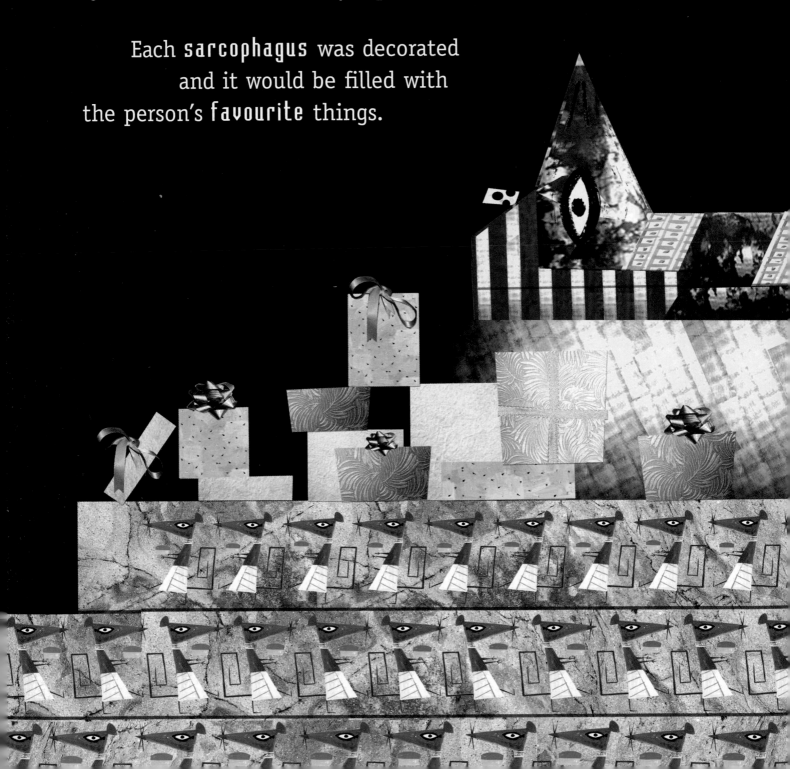

I think it would be nice
to make one for
Nibbles... because he was
REALLY special."

Lola says,
    "Yes, Nibbles was
completely DEFINITELY
    very special."

So we decorate a special **shoebox** for Nibbles.
And we put all his favourite things into it.

Lola says, "Nibbles loved glitter...

and he loved **leaves**,

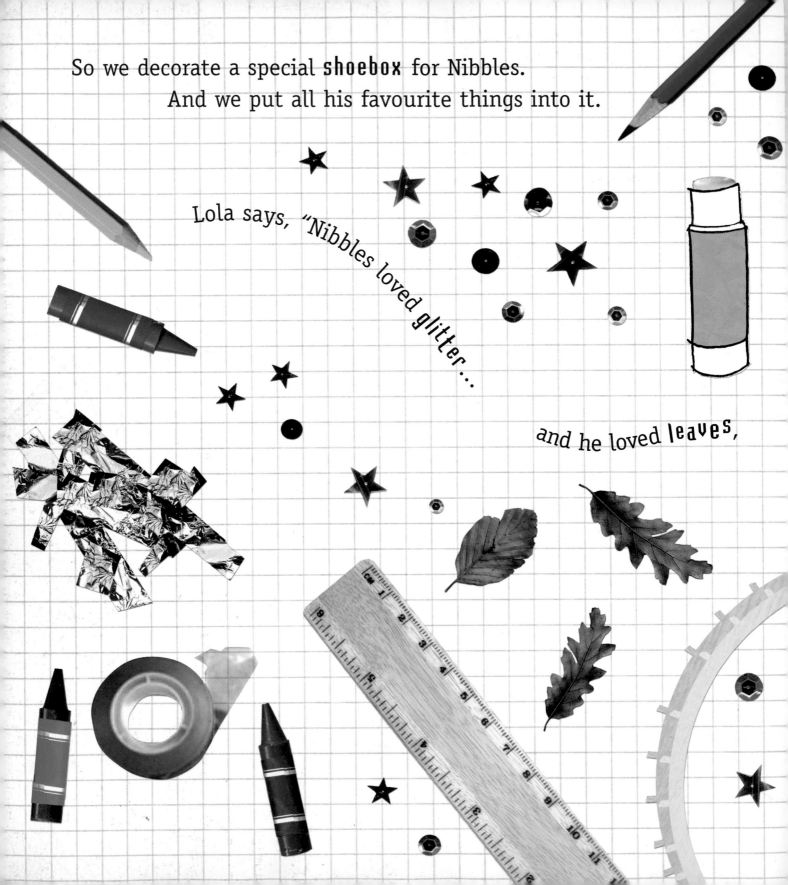

... and he **really** loved his wheel.

And this was
his favourite s0ck."

"Hey, that's MY s0ck!" I say.

But Lola says,
"No, Charlie.
That was Nibbles's
favouritest s0ck."

Later, Mum puts Nibbles in the special **box**
we made and Dad digs a hole in the garden,
in a really **nice** place by the tree.

I say, "Nibbles, you were a very clever mouse and I didn't really mind about you **nibbling** everything."

And Lola says, "I will not EVER **never** FORGET you, **nibbles.**"

A couple of weeks later, we go to
Marv's house to see his new **mouse**.
It's called **Squeak**.

I say, "Maybe WE should
get another **mouse**, Lola?"

But Lola says, "No, Charlie.
I will be very EXTREMELY **upset** in case
the next mouse dies too."

Marv says, "All mice die, Lola.
   Because, you see, they don't
live for a very long time."

But then we see Lola isn't listening.

Instead she says,
"Charlie! Did you see what Squeak did?
He jumped all the way from HERE
to all the way over THERE!"

I say,
"Nibbles never did jumping, did he, Lola?"

And Lola says,
"Maybe perhaps we
should get ANOTHER
mouse after all."

So Lola decides to get a **mouse** of her own.

"Ohh," I say. "What is his name, Lola?"

And Lola says, "Tickles!"